Fields of Follies

PLANET
ADVENTURE

Mark E. Hefferan

To order additional copies of this book, contact:
Xlibris
844-714-8691
www.Xlibris.com
Orders@Xlibris.com

ISBN: Softcover   978-1-6641-8379-7
        Hardcover   978-1-6641-8380-3
        EBook   978-1-6641-8378-0

Library of Congress Control Number: 2021913883

Print information available on the last page

Rev. date: 07/14/2021

For my nephews, Bradlee, Nathan, and Ryan
and for my niece, Rachel.
Hope you enjoy the book!

Acknowledgements

Special thanks to Svitlana Vivchar, Becky Ross Michael, Gerard and Theresa Hefferan. It was a pleasure working on this project, and without all of you, this would not be possible.

In a distant world, somewhere in the Milky Way galaxy, there exists the *Fields of Follies*. It has lush green grass, rolling hills, clear blue streams, and three best friends: a penguin, rabbit and cuckoo bird. How they got here is unknown, and how long it has existed will also bring wonder.

Ace, Ely ("L-E"), and Tictok want to venture out into this vast yet lonely universe, to find new life and hopefully more friends.

This is their story.

ACE

ELY

TICTOK

"Tictok, are you home?" calls Ely. An answering chirp from the bird assures him that all is well. "Let's go see how Ace is doing on building the spacecraft for our adventure."

In excitement, they follow the trail together, knowing the project is nearly complete. Soon they will be able to explore the far reaches of space to find new friends.

"Hello, Ace," Ely says as they approach the spacecraft worksite.

"Good morning," answers the penguin. "I'm just finishing up some final touches on the undercarriage before the job is complete. One last piece needs to be put in place. And then a bolt must be tightened inside, under the control panel."

Ace's black-and-white feathers emerge from underneath the machine. He waddles inside the cockpit to tighten up that last bolt.

"I forgot my wrench, Ely. Could you please pass that to me?" he asks.

The rabbit grabs a wrench from the table and climbs aboard the spacecraft, handing Ace his tool. Tictok lands on a chair to watch.

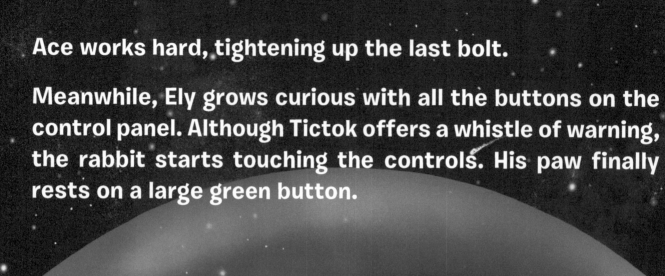

Ace works hard, tightening up the last bolt.

Meanwhile, Ely grows curious with all the buttons on the control panel. Although Tictok offers a whistle of warning, the rabbit starts touching the controls. His paw finally rests on a large green button.

ACTIVATE

Ely realizes too late that he has activated the spacecraft. The glass door closes with a loud swish.

"What did you do!" yells a frightened Ace. "What have you touched!" he adds, his eyes quickly scanning the panel. Ely remains speechless.

Before anything can be done, they hear an ear-splitting roar. The three are pushed back into their seats with more force than they could have imagined. They are leaving the Fields of Follies and taking flight!

The three friends find themselves crash-landed in the ice fields of the planet Pluto. They all hop out, disoriented but unharmed. Tictok points at the flakes of red snow and a beautiful landscape of icy mountains.

"Looks lovely, but the weather feels extremely cold here," says Ace.

"I thought penguins liked cold weather," Ely answers.

"Yes, but the chance of finding new friends here is impossible. We best get out of the ice and be on our way."

After traveling for some time, the three notice a rather large planet in the distance.

"Look!" shouts Ely. "This one has big bright rings surrounding it!"

"I'm flying us in for a closer look," says Ace. Their craft flies directly through the rings and arrives at the planet Saturn.

"There's nowhere to land here!" Ace yells. The winds are unbearable, and the yellow gas clouds make visibility nearly impossible.

"Guess we're in trouble?" asks Ely as Tictok whistles in agreement.

Using all his skills, Ace steers the harsh surroundings. Shaken up, they continue onward in their search.

After hurtling through space for some time, Ace, Ely and Tictok finally see Neptune outside the window.

"It's like a giant blue ball," notes Ely with a twitch of his nose.

Excited about the discovery, they decide to go in for a closer look.

"I thought this planet's atmosphere might be okay," says Ace, "but it's becoming unbelievably windy."

"What's that?" shouts Ely after something catches his eye. "It looks to be raining bright, shiny diamonds!" Amazed by how beautiful the rocks look, Ely grabs an empty sack from underneath the seat and opens the canopy to fill his bag.

"It's impossible to land our spacecraft on this gas giant with no solid ground," says Ace. "Guess we won't find any new friends here either," he adds in disappointment.

Ely is at least happy about the shiny rocks he has collected to take back home. Ace engages the spacecraft and pushes their way out of Neptune into a new direction.

After traveling for a long time, they notice more light than they have ever seen since leaving the Fields of Follies.

"What's going on?" asks Ely.

"It must be the Sun!" Ace guesses. "And look, there's a small planet hovering around it."

"It's starting to feel really hot," Ely notices.

"Yes, with this intense heat, we better land on the dark side of that planet," suggests Ace.

Ace pilots their craft a bit closer to the planet Mercury where there is a bit of light without being exposed directly to the Sun. This is where it is a more comfortably warm zone.

"We've been roaming around for quite a while and found nothing," Ace points out. "And the Sun is creeping faster around the edge of this place. I'm scared of the overwhelming heat coming our way. We need to blast off this desolate planet before it's too late."

"I'll take your word for it," Ely agrees with a twitch of his whiskers.

Disappointed but not giving up, the three friends continue their journey. They whiz past asteroids and gaze out into deep space.

"Wow, this is amazing!" says Ely in awe.

"Even better yet, look over there," calls Ace, lifting a flipper to point.

Once again, they have stumbled upon something massive! This is the biggest of all planets they have seen. It is the planet Jupiter.

"Yippee!" calls Ely. "It's so big."

"This planet does look huge, but we're not sure to find any friends here." Ace replies.

As they pass by all the small moons of Jupiter, the three notice a large red spot. "We'll travel in that direction to check it out," decides Ace.

Before long, Ely yells, "What's happening?"

"The gravity is pulling us into the giant red spot," says Ace. "There's a furious storm going on. Hang on to your seats. This is going to be a wild ride!" Tictok chatters in fear, looking back and forth between his friends.

Inside the storm, Ace loses all control of the spacecraft. "Oh no!" The winds are so strong, and he has no visibility or chance to navigate. Luckily for them, Jupiter is also a gas giant, and there is no place for them to crash.

The constant storm tosses them around for hours.

"I think we're going to be okay," Ace finally says.

The three travelers are being thrown toward the Northern Hemisphere and making their way through the northern lights of Jupiter.

"Yay, we're finally free," Ely cheers. "But will we ever find other life-forms like us?"

"I'm wondering the same thing," agrees Ace. After what feels like an eternity, they stumble upon the faint green of the planet Uranus.

"Looks like an ice giant," Ace says in a disgruntled voice."I already know there isn't anyone living here based on what we've seen on other icy planets."

"Let's fly in and check it out anyway," insists Ely.

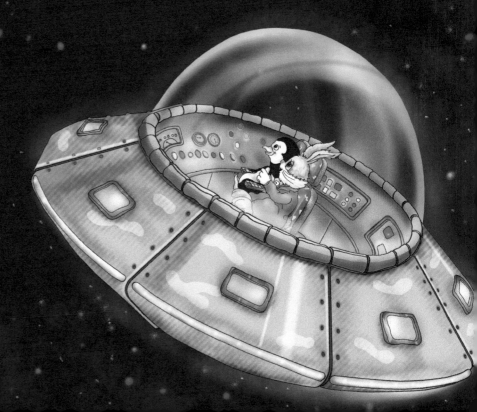

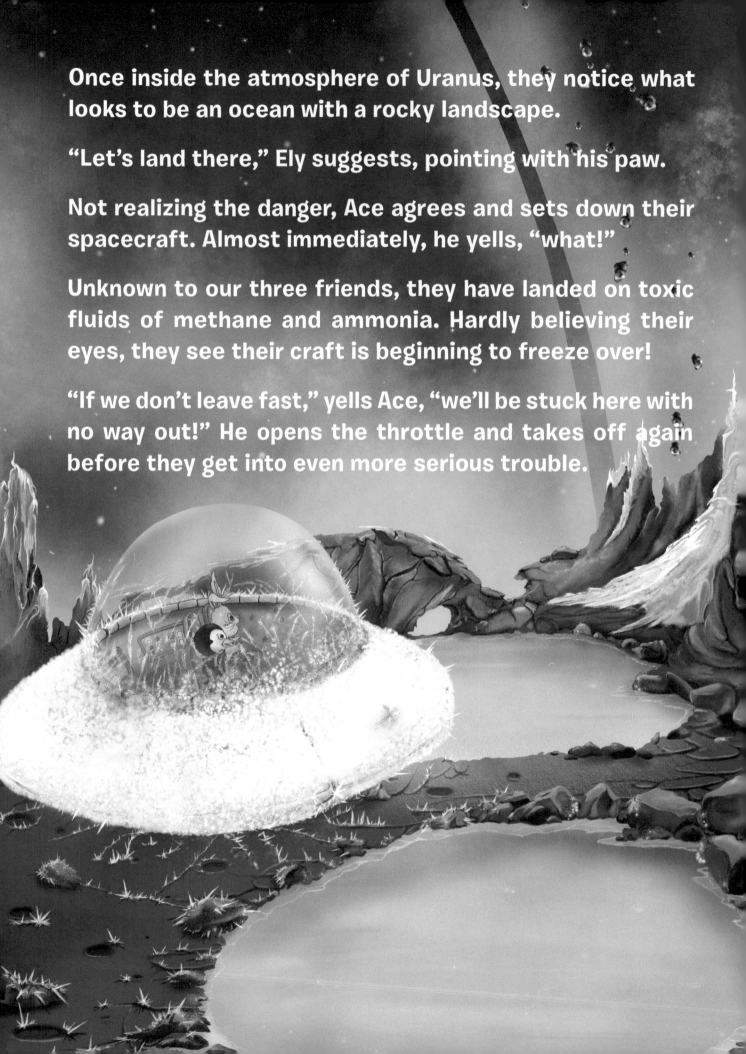

Once inside the atmosphere of Uranus, they notice what looks to be an ocean with a rocky landscape.

"Let's land there," Ely suggests, pointing with his paw.

Not realizing the danger, Ace agrees and sets down their spacecraft. Almost immediately, he yells, "what!"

Unknown to our three friends, they have landed on toxic fluids of methane and ammonia. Hardly believing their eyes, they see their craft is beginning to freeze over!

"If we don't leave fast," yells Ace, "we'll be stuck here with no way out!" He opens the throttle and takes off again before they get into even more serious trouble.

"Will we ever find anyone or anything?" asks Ely after they are safely away from Uranus.

"I'm starting to question the same thing," Ace says. "But I have no intentions of giving up yet. Are you with me?" Ely and Tictok both nod in agreement, so on they continue, traveling through the depths of the universe.

"Another planet," Ely finally calls, wiggling his ears at the yellowish-white form of Venus in the distance.

"Yup, let's go," Ace tells his friends.

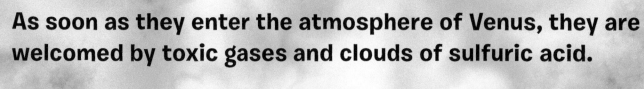

As soon as they enter the atmosphere of Venus, they are welcomed by toxic gases and clouds of sulfuric acid.

"It's turning really hot in here again," Ely notices.

"And I'm having trouble steering with this heavy pressure," says Ace. "I'm going to land us over there, near that volcanic mountain."

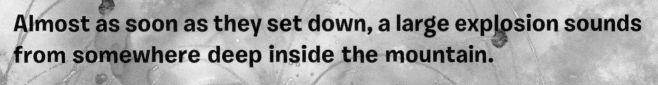

Almost as soon as they set down, a large explosion sounds from somewhere deep inside the mountain.

"Lava!" yells Ely, who points with a shaking paw.

Ace immediately takes off again. "I dislike admitting defeat," he says, "but I think we need to fly back home to the Fields of Follies."

"I suppose you're right," answers Ely, "but I'm sure disappointed. We still didn't find any new friends!"

Tictok lets out a mournful cry.

The ride toward home is quiet and feels exhausting. Gazing out the window, they suddenly see the bright red of Mars.

"Huh," Ely mutters. "That's one we haven't seen before."

"Let's give it one last chance," says Ace with some hope in his voice.

As they descend toward Mars, a dusty red cold planet, they see something new and strange.

"I think it's a robot!" Ace cries. In utter excitement, Ace, Ely and Tictok land on Mars. Ace waddles from the spacecraft first, followed by Ely, who arrives outside in one big hop. Tictok hovers above them, with small wings flapping.

All three greet the robot with joy and curiosity. What they do not know is that this robot has been sent to Mars from the people of planet Earth!

Back on Earth, cheers erupt in the space control center. While viewing the surroundings through the eyes of their robot, the control workers believe they are seeing aliens who live on Mars. In awe, they decide to send astronauts to investigate their findings.

Back on Mars, Ace, Ely and Tictok are so happy to have found something like a new friend. They follow the robot around Mars for several months, even riding on its back.

"What's that?" asks Ely one day. "Are my eyes playing tricks on me?"

"No, I see it too," answers Ace. "It looks like another spaceship!"

Excited and nervous, the three companions get off the robot and watch as the spaceship from Earth touches down near them on Mars. All three friends look on in amazement.

The door of the spaceship slides open, and two astronauts walk down the stairs into the mist.

To be continued ...

CPSIA information can be obtained
at www.ICGtesting.com
Printed in the USA
LVHW052340090921
697463LV00002B/20

9 781664 183797